# MY FIRST
# PHONICS
# DICTIONARY

Lynne Blanton, Ph.D.

Consultant: Carole Palmer

Publications International, Ltd.

**Lynne Blanton, Ph.D.,** has been a writer and editor with Creative Services Associates, Inc., a developer of educational materials, for more than 20 years. She also worked as an editor at Rand McNally and the Riverside Publishing Company and has a B.A. in English and history from Birmingham-Southern College and a Ph.D. in communications from the University of Illinois.

**CONSULTANT: Carole Palmer** holds an M.A. in reading. Previously a first grade teacher, she currently writes and reviews educational materials, including reading, phonics, and spelling projects, for children at all grade levels. She is the founder and president of Creative Services Associates, Inc.

Front cover: PIL Collection, Shutterstock

Back cover: Shutterstock

Image Sources: Artville, Brand X Pictures, Chrysler Group Media, Dreamstime, Image Club, Photodisc, PIL Collection, Sacco Productions Limited/Chicago, Shutterstock, Thinkstock

Illustrations: Bill Petersen

Louis Weber, CEO
Publications International, Ltd.
7373 North Cicero Avenue
Lincolnwood, Illinois 60712

ISBN-13: 978-1-4508-1480-5
ISBN-10: 1-4508-1480-8

Manufactured in China.

8 7 6 5 4 3 2 1

# Contents

## Vowel Sounds

## More Consonant Sounds

## More Vowel Sounds

# Let's Get Started!

*My First Phonics Dictionary* offers an organized, understandable, and engaging way to learn about phonics, or the relationships between letters and sounds in English. This book is designed to make phonics easy and fun for beginning learners and for the parents and teachers who help them. The sooner young children start learning about letters and sounds, the better prepared and the more successful they will be when they start learning to read in school. Research supports this point: Children with a phonics background are a step ahead.

## Letters

Do your children know the letters of the alphabet? You can use page 7 of *My First Phonics Dictionary* and the following activities to check their ability to name the letters.

- Point to a letter on the page and ask your children to name it. Say a letter name and ask your children to point to the letter on the page.
- Sing "The Alphabet Song" with your children. Take turns pointing to the letters on page 7 as you sing the song.

- Write the letters on index cards or scraps of paper to make alphabet cards. Ask your children to match the letters on the alphabet cards to the letters on page 7 as they say the letter names.

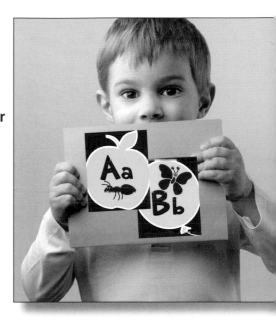

- Mix the alphabet cards and spread them out on a table. Point to a letter on page 7 and ask your children to name the letter and then find the alphabet card with the same letter.

## Sounds

Once your children can recognize the letters of the alphabet, move on to the sounds that go with them: It's time for phonics.

English uses 26 letters: 21 consonants (*b, c, d, f, g, h, j, k, l, m, n, p, q, r, s, t, v, w, x, y, z*) and 5 vowels (*a, e, i, o, u*). However, English has more than 26 sounds because many of the letters, particularly the vowels, can stand for more than one sound. *My First Phonics Dictionary* presents 38 sounds, 25 for consonants and 13 for vowels. While there are more sounds, these 38 provide the best foundation for children who are just beginning to learn about phonics.

## Using This Book

Turn to the table of contents, and you'll see that this book is divided into four sections. The simpler consonant and vowel sounds are presented in the first two sections, "Consonant Sounds" and "Vowel Sounds." The more difficult consonant and vowel sounds are presented in the last two sections, "More Consonant Sounds" and "More Vowel Sounds." The Sounds Chart at the end of the book is a handy reference that lists the key pictures, key words, and other words used for each sound in the book.

Now let's see how a sound is presented in *My First Phonics Dictionary*. Turn to pages 8 and 9. At the top of the first page is the key picture and picture name (or key word). When you name the key picture and say *bear,* you hear the *b* sound (/b/) at the beginning. The red letter *b* at the beginning of the key word *bear* tells you that *b* stands for /b/. The other pictures and words on pages 8 and 9 offer more examples of the same letter-sound relationship.

Follow these steps the first time you and your children share these pages:

- Say the key word, emphasizing the beginning sound, /b/ /b/ /b/ *bear,* and ask your children to do the same. Point to the letter *b* and ask your children to identify it. Tell them the letter *b* spells the /b/ sound in *bear.*
- Compare the key word *bear* to each of the other picture names (for example, **b**ear-**b**ike or **b**ear-**b**ook), emphasizing the beginning sounds in both words. Ask your children whether the beginning sounds they hear are the same. Then ask them what letter stands for that sound.

Use the same process to introduce each of the sounds in *My First Phonics Dictionary*. Remember to always tie the sound your children hear to the letter (or letters) that spell the sound.

You can use *My First Phonics Dictionary* in many ways, depending on the ages and interests of your children. After you introduce a sound, say one of the given words and ask your children to point to the word or to the picture for the word. Or point to a word or picture and ask your children to say the word or name the picture. In turn, encourage your children to ask you to identify letters, sounds, and pictures as you learn about phonics together.

# The Alphabet Sounds

cat   ball   can   dog   hen

fox   gorilla   hippo   pig   jam

koala   lamp   mug   nest   lock

pillow   quail   rabbit   socks   turkey

drum   vase   watch   box   yo-yo

zebra

**bear** **b /b/**

bike

book

bat

ball

**box**

**boy**

**bed**

**boat**

**monkey   m /m/**

**moon**

**map**

**mouse**

**man**

**mask**

**milk**

**mug**

**mop**

**pig    p /p/**

**pen**

**pail**

**pan**

**pear**

**pillow**

**pin**

**pencil**

**peach**

**dog     d /d/**

**door**

**desk**

**dish**

**deer**

dime

doll

duck

dig

**gift**

**goat**    **g /g/**

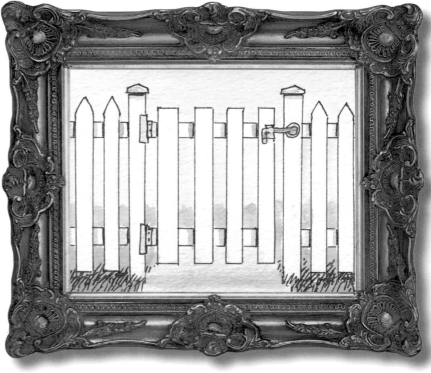

**girl**          **gate**

**gum**

**game**

**gorilla**

monkey

mouse

boy

gate

ball

dog

bear

man

goat

pail

pig

duck

PARK ZOO

19

**jet    j /j/**

**jar**

**jam**

**jeans**

**jacket**

**jacks**

**Jeep®**

**lion** l /l/

**lock**

**leaf**

**ladder**

**lamp**

**lake**

**log**

**lamb**

**letters**

net    n /n/

nine

nest

nickel

nail

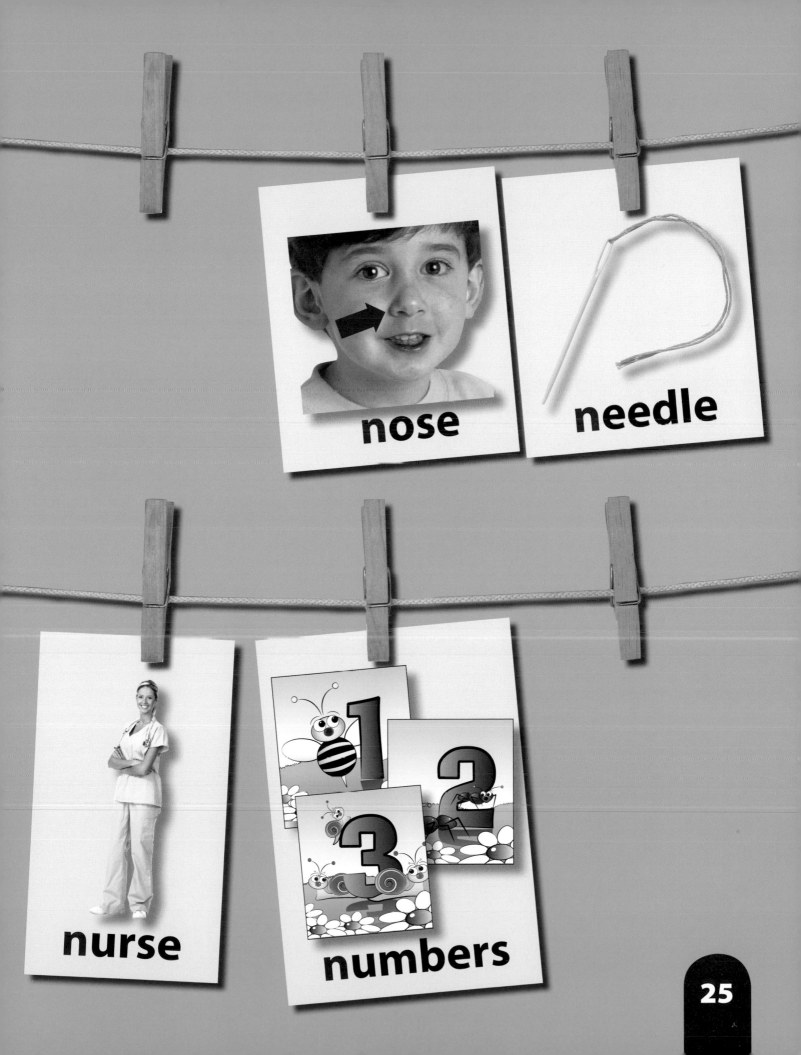

**nose**

**needle**

**nurse**

**numbers**

25

**tiger**   **t /t/**

**top**

**turkey**

**ten**

**turtle**

**tire**

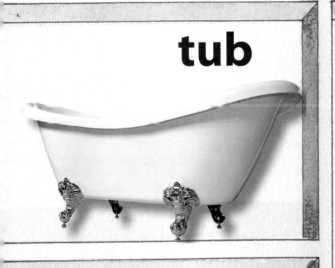

**table**

**tub**

**tent**

**fox f /f/**

**fish**

**four**

**fan**

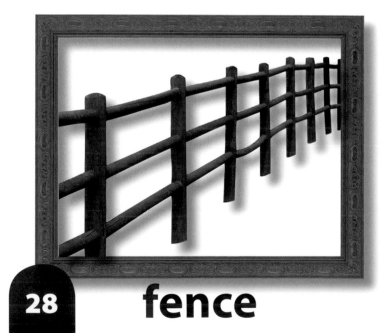

**fence**

**fork**

**five**

**feather**

**fire**

29

# Let's Review!

lion

leopard

fish

turtle

30 net

tent

Jeep®

fire

nest

feather

leaf

seal    s /s/

soap

six

saw

sun

**7**

**seven**

**socks**

**sail**

**sand**

**vase   v /v/**

**vet**

**van**

**vine**

**vest**

**vacuum**

**violin**

**horse    h /h/**

**hat**

**hammer**

**house**

**hand**

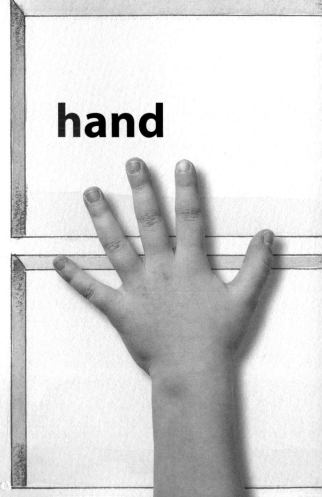

**hippo**

**hay**

**hill**

**hose**

kite

king  k /k/

kitten

**koala**

**key**

**kit**

**kangaroo**

**rabbit**   r /r/

**ring**

**ruler**

**rake**

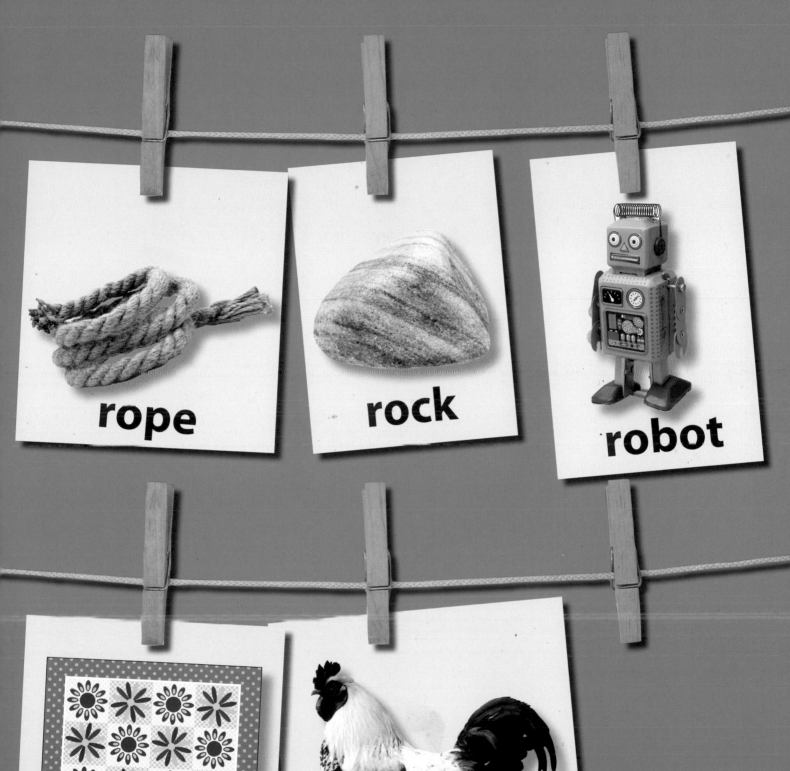

**rope**

**rock**

**robot**

**rug**

**rooster**

sail

kite

seal

rock

**Let's Review!**

key

42

sun

house

hill

van

vine

rope

43

## wagon  w /w/

### watch

## wolf

## worm

## watermelon

44

**wing**

**web**

**well**

**window**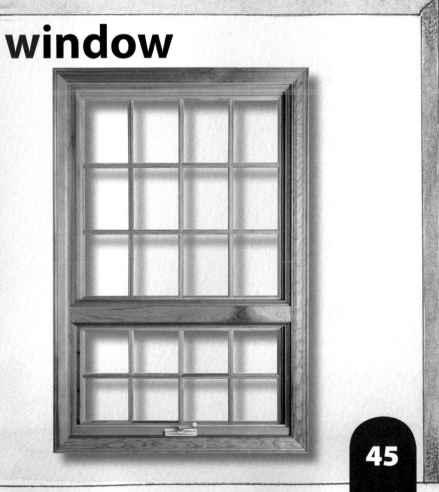

45

cat    c /k/

cap

car

coat

can

comb

computer

candle

cow

**yarn y /y/**

**yellow**

**yawn**

**yard**

**yell**

**yak**

**yo-yo**

**queen   qu /kw/**

**quarter**

**quiet**

**quail**

**quill**

quack!

**quack**

**question**

**quilt**

51

**zebra    z /z/**

**zipper**

**zoo**

**zoom**

**zero**

**fox** **x /ks/**

**box**

**six**

**mix**

**ox**

quail

zero

CORN
6 for
$1.00

car

fox

worm

55

**cat**   a /a/

**hat**

**can**

**lamp**

**map**

flag

fan

crab

bat

57

**hen    e /e/**

**bed**

**pen**

**web**

**nest**

**10**

ten

shell

desk

jet

**pig    i /i/**

**crib**

**fish**

**swing**

**six**

**dish**

**pin**

**ring**

**quilt**

fox   o /o/

clock

doll

mop

**pot**

**lock**

**box**

**knot**

**top**

**drum**

**duck   u /u/**

**rug**

**bus**

**tub**

**truck**

**sun**

# Let's Review!

map

clock

pen

fish

nest

66

flag

today's number is

six

6

fan

drum

box

rug

desk

67

**chick   ch /ch/**

**chimney**

**chain**

**chair**

**children**

**cheese**

**chest**

**cherries**

**chin**

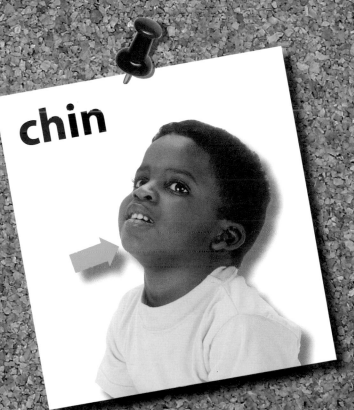

**sheep   sh /sh/**

**shell**

**ship**

**shovel**

**shoes**

**shirt**

**shark**

**shower**

**shelf**

71

**thumb   th /th/**

**thirty**

**thorn**

**thermometer**

72

**thirteen**

**thimble**

**third**

**whale   wh /hw/**

**wheel**

**wheat**

whisper

white

whistle

whiskers

shark

children

shirt

shell

shoes

77

**snake a_e /ā/**

**gate**

**whale**

**vase**

**cane**

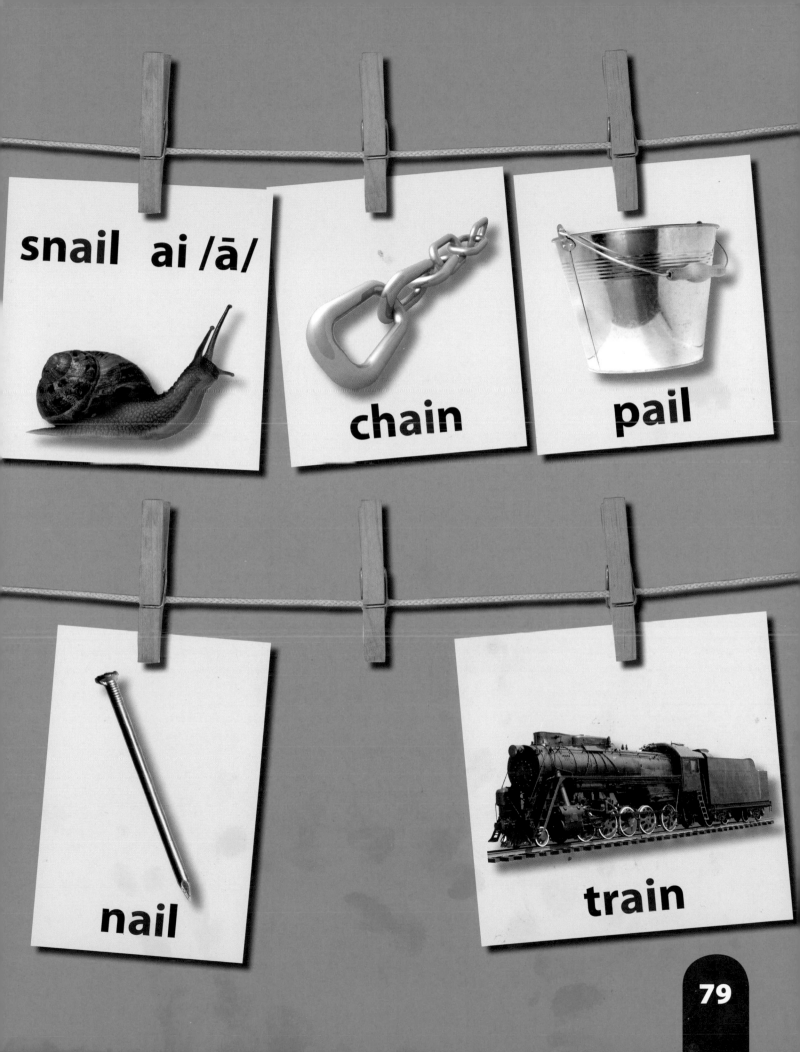

snail ai /ā/

chain

pail

nail

train

**seal  ea /ē/**

**leaf**

**peach**

**read**

**jeans**

**sheep** ee /ē/

**cheese**

**three**

3

**wheel**

**queen**

# bike   i_e /ī/

kite

mice

bride

**5**
five

slide

vine

**9**
nine

dime

**rose   o_e /ō/**

**phone**

**nose**

**globe**

**rope**

84

boat    oa /ō/

toad

goat

soap

coat

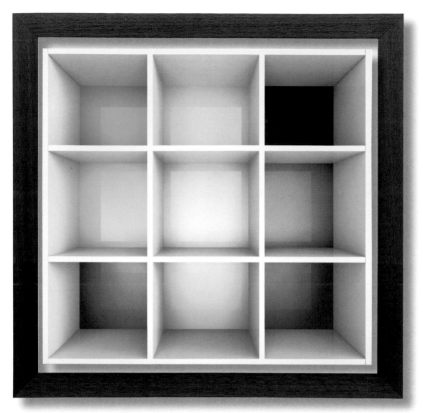

**cube   u_e /ū/**

**cute**

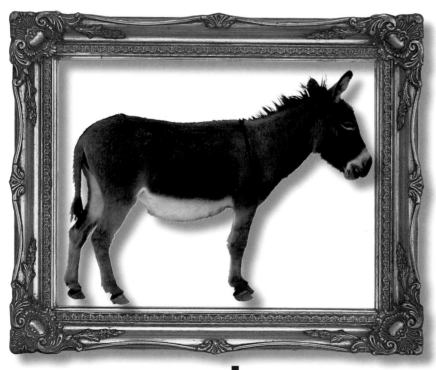

**mule**

**huge**

**bugle    u /ū/**

**music**

**uniform**

**menu**

**car    ar /är/**

**yarn**

**cart**

**stars**

**shark**

horse     or /ôr/

corn

fork

porch

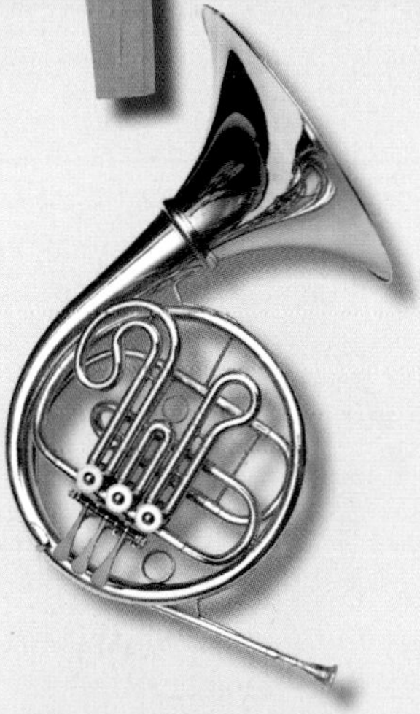

horn

**bird**   **ir /ûr/**

**circle**

**thirty**

**30**

**girl**

**shirt**

**turtle**

**purse**

**fern**

**herd**

**purple**  ur /ûr/

**perch**  er /ûr/

fern

kite

stars

jeans

coat

train

bugle

cube

horse

girl

bride

globe

queen

snake

turtle

93

# Sounds Chart

## Consonant Sounds

| Letter(s) & Sound | Key Picture & Word | More Words |
|---|---|---|
| b /b/ | bear | bike, book, bat, ball, box, bed, boat, boy |
| c /k/ | cat | cat, car, coat, can, comb, cow, candle, computer |
| d /d/ | dog | door, desk, dish, deer, dime, doll, duck, dig |
| f /f/ | fox | fish, four, fan, fence, five, fork, feather, fire |
| g /g/ | goat | girl, gate, gift, gum, game, gorilla |
| h /h/ | horse | hat, house, hammer, hand, hippo, hose, hay, hill |
| j /j/ | jet | jar, jacks, Jeep®, jacket, jam, jeans |
| k /k/ | king | kite, key, kitten, kit, koala, kangaroo |
| l /l/ | lion | lock, lamp, ladder, leaf, log, lake, lamb, letters |
| m /m/ | monkey | moon, mask, man, map, mop, milk, mug, mouse |
| n /n/ | net | nine, nest, nail, nickel, nose, needle, numbers, nurse |
| p /p/ | pig | pan, pail, pen, pillow, pin, pear, peach, pencil |
| qu /kw/ | queen | quarter, quill, quilt, quack, quiet, question, quail |

| Letter(s) & Sound | Key Picture & Word | More Words |
|---|---|---|
| r /r/ | rabbit | rake, rock, rug, rope, ring, ruler, rooster, robot |
| s /s/ | seal | soap, sun, saw, six, seven, socks, sand, sail |
| t /t/ | tiger | top, turtle, turkey, ten, table, tire, tub, tent |
| v /v/ | vase | van, vest, vet, vine, violin, vacuum |
| w /w/ | wagon | watch, window, worm, web, well, watermelon, wolf, wing |
| x /ks/ | fox | box, six, mix, ox |
| y /y/ | yarn | yo-yo, yard, yell, yak, yawn, yellow |
| z /z/ | zebra | zipper, zoo, zero, zoom |
| ch /ch/ | chick | chair, chin, cheese, chimney, chest, chain, cherries, children |
| sh /sh/ | sheep | shoes, shovel, ship, shell, shirt, shark, shelf, shower |
| th /th/ | thumb | thirteen, thorn, thermometer, thirty, thimble, third |
| wh /hw/ | whale | wheel, whistle, whisper, whiskers, white, wheat |

# Vowel Sounds

| Letter(s) & Sound | Key Picture(s) & Word(s) | More Words |
|---|---|---|
| a /a/ | cat | hat, flag, map, can, lamp, fan, bat, crab |
| e /e/ | hen | bed, web, pen, nest, ten, shell, desk, jet |
| i /i/ | pig | fish, ring, six, pin, dish, swing, quilt, crib |
| o /o/ | fox | mop, clock, doll, pot, box, lock, top, knot |
| u /u/ | duck | bus, drum, tub, sun, rug, truck |
| a_e, ai /ā/ | snail  snake | vase, cane, gate, whale chain, pail, nail, train |
| ea, ee /ē/ | seal  sheep | leaf, jeans, peach, read cheese, wheel, three, queen |
| i_e /ī/ | bike | kite, mice, nine, bride, dime, five, vine, slide |
| o_e, oa /ō/ | rose  boat | phone, globe, rope, nose coat, soap, toad, goat |
| u_e, u /ū/ | cube  bugle | mule, cute, huge music, uniform, menu |
| ar /är/ | car | yarn, cart, stars, shark |
| or /ôr/ | horse | fork, corn, horn, porch |
| ir, ur, er /ûr/ | bird  purple  perch | girl, shirt, circle, thirty purse, turtle fern, herd |